P9-DMZ-645
BIONICLE®
Ex-Library: Friends of
Lake County Public Library
Prisoners of the Pit

BIONICLE®

FIND THE POWER,

LIVE THE LEGEND

The legend comes alive in these exciting BIONICLE® books:

BIONICLE Chronicles
#1 Tale of the Toa
#2 Beware the Bohrok
#3 Makuta's Revenge
#4 Tales of the Masks

BIONICLE: Mask of Light
The Official Guide to BIONICLE
BIONICLE Collector's Sticker Book
BIONICLE: Metru Nui: City of Legends
BIONICLE: Rahi Beasts
BIONICLE: Dark Hunters
BIONICLE: World

BIONICLE Adventures
#1 Mystery of Metru Nui
#2 Trial by Fire
#3 The Darkness Below
#4 Legends of Metru Nui
#5 Voyage of Fear
#6 Maze of Shadows
#7 Web of the Visorak
#8 Challenge of the Hordika
#9 Web of Shadows
#10 Time Trap

BIONICLE Legends
#1 Island of Doom
#2 Dark Destiny
#3 Power Play
#4 Legacy of Evil
#5 Inferno
#6 City of the Lost

BIONICLE®

Prisoners of the Pit

by Greg Farshtey

SCHOLASTIC INC.
New York Toronto London Auckland Sydney
Mexico City New Delhi Hong Kong Buenos Aires

For Tim, who helps make any Pit bearable

ISBN-13: 978-0-439-89034-2
ISBN-10: 0-439-89034-9

12 11 10 9 8 7 6 5 4 8 9 10 11/0

Printed in the U.S.A.
First printing, July 2007

PROLOGUE

A formless wisp of greenish-black smoke slipped silently through a tunnel made of stone. To anyone watching, it might have seemed like a cloud of oddly colored dust, and no more. But if they could have sensed the malevolent intelligence that drove its seemingly random movements, they would have fled in horror.

The Matoran villagers of the island of Voya Nui had known this hated substance by the name "antidermis." The evil Piraka who had seized control of their island had used it to enslave most of the population, before finally being defeated by a team of heroic Toa. The crystal vat that contained the antidermis was smashed in battle, and the substance was scattered into the air.

But this was not the end. The tremendous

willpower behind the antidermis forced its molecules to come back together. Now it was again whole — yet far from complete.

Once, in another place and time, the antidermis had been known by another name. Then it was housed inside black armor, its essence concealed by an infamous mask of power. Just as now, it was the intellect, the memories, the twisted ambitions, and the very life force of a legendary being.

He was called Makuta.

Hungry for power and worship, he had led his Brotherhood in a rebellion against the Great Spirit Mata Nui and actually defeated that mighty entity. But his plans extended far beyond just one victory. His continued pursuit of his goals led to an encounter with a Toa of Light, during which his armor was shattered. The armor was no longer able to contain his energies, causing them to leak out into the atmosphere.

Frustrated, but not defeated, Makuta had influenced the Piraka to seek out the object of power he needed: the Mask of Life. For a time, it looked like his pawns would succeed, until Toa once again interfered.

First the Rahi beasts of Mata Nui, then the Bohrok swarms, Makuta thought as his essence drifted through the tunnels. *Now the Piraka. When will I learn to stop working my will through others? All other beings are weak and pathetic fools who cannot begin to comprehend my plans. I, and I alone, must take matters in hand if my grand design is to succeed. There are obstacles, of course — there always are. The Mask of Life is not a prize easily won. But this game I play now is different from all others . . . and this time I cannot lose, for my longtime enemies will be my unwitting champions.*

A soft sound touched the minds of those who fought in the tunnels, so gently that they dismissed it as a trick of the senses. It was the sound of Makuta's laughter.

The Toa will get the Mask of Life for me . . . and doom their own kind in the process, thought the master of shadows. *And what a perfect revenge that will be.*

ONE

Toa Inika Kongu dove out of the way as a wickedly curved dagger flew overhead. Looking up, he saw the blade had buried itself in the rock, about where his head had been a moment before.

"Just once — just once! — I'd like to take a trip-walk without someone trying to kill me!" he said.

Toa Inika Jaller ran past, stopped, turned, and fired a blast of fire from his sword. He aimed over the head of his scale-skinned pursuers, hoping to scare them off. It didn't work. It would have failed even if he had aimed to burn them down. Driven by hatred and a need for vengeance, nothing was going to stop these Zyglak.

The battle was one more nightmare in a journey that had been filled with them. The Toa

Inika had come to the island of Voya Nui in search of six other heroes, the Toa Nuva, who had disappeared there. They found themselves in a battle with villains who had seized control of the island and were seeking the powerful Kanohi Mask of Life which was hidden there.

In the end, the Inika had won the fight, found the mask, and the Toa Nuva had been rescued. But a last blow struck by their enemies cost them their grip on the mask, and it plunged beneath the ocean waves. Their only hope of retrieving it was to journey through a labyrinth of stone tunnels that extended from Voya Nui down to the ocean depths. Once there, they would have to find some way to locate the mask and get it back, not easy when some of them were poor swimmers and none could breathe underwater.

Of course, first they had to get there. As they moved through the twisted and narrow tunnels, the Toa quickly discovered they weren't alone. The labyrinth was home to a race of warriors with a murderous grudge against Toa, Matoran, and anyone else associated with the

Great Spirit Mata Nui. The running battle that followed had been violent and frightening, and had revealed things about the Toa themselves that they might have preferred not to face.

Right now, though, the Toa were just hoping to still have all their parts intact when this was over. More Zyglak were emerging from every side tunnel, their knives and spears flying through the air like angry swamp hornets. Worse, everything their blades struck was instantly destroyed.

"I hear water up ahead!" Toa Inika Hahli shouted. She was barely able to keep moving, having been wounded badly in an earlier battle.

The six Toa Inika rounded a bend in the tunnel and then stopped dead. There was a large gap in the stone wall, through which ocean water flooded in. The passages up ahead were already underwater.

"Anybody have a Toa canister in their pack?" asked Toa Inika Hewkii. "I didn't think so. We might have stronger lungs than most, but that's a lot of water out there."

A hail of spears clattered against the stone wall just behind the Toa, eating holes in the rock. "And that's a lot of Zyglak back there," said Toa Inika Nuparu. "Looks like the last one in the pool is skewered meat."

A violent tremor suddenly shook the tunnels. Cracks appeared in the walls, and fragments of stone fell from the ceiling. It seemed as if something was trying to crush the entire labyrinth from the outside, and doing a great job of it, too.

The Zyglak looked around frantically as their world threatened to collapse. For the moment, the Toa were forgotten.

"Let's move!" said Jaller. "We'll take our chances in the ocean."

"Hold on," said Hewkii. "I like a challenge as much as the next Toa, but — Toa of Stone, remember? Even with a few lessons in my Matoran days, I still swim like a stone."

The tunnels shook again, worse this time, as if they were being wrenched from side to side. Now the Zyglak were fleeing in sheer terror.

"Whatever's out there can't be worse than what's in here," Jaller replied. "I'll light up my swords — if they burn hot enough, they'll stay lit underwater. Follow my light — maybe we can find an air pocket."

Jaller took a deep breath and dove through the gap in the wall. The other Toa Inika followed. Hahli sensed immediately something was not right about the water. It wasn't the kind found around the island of Mata Nui, or the smooth liquid protodermis that surrounded the island of Metru Nui. Water, by its nature, was a force of life and healing — but this liquid felt foul and destructive, like it had somehow been corrupted.

There wasn't time to puzzle it out now. Jaller's burning swords had revealed the source of the tremors in the tunnels: a massive undersea creature wrapped around the stone cord that led from Voya Nui down here. It was trying to crush the cord, and the tunnels inside it, in its coils. Then its huge, serpentine head looked in the Toa's direction. It had spotted Jaller's flames.

Light! The creature knew that light meant living things, and living things meant a meal. It uncoiled its 300-foot-long body from the cord and started for the source of the illumination.

Jaller and the other Toa saw the monster's shadowy form heading for them. They braced for an attack, knowing the battle would probably use up the air in their lungs and doom them. But the huge serpent was not going to give them any choice in the matter.

Then the world went white. Blindingly, overwhelmingly white, a blazing illumination that seared the eyes and tore at the mind and body. The Toa screamed from shock and pain, even though it meant water would fill their straining lungs. The creature above them reeled as waves of energy ripped through the water.

In the midst of the agony, the Toa heard a voice. It wasn't speaking words so much as conveying a primal emotion, but somehow they all knew who was "speaking." It was the Kanohi Mask of Life, the artifact they sought, and it was calling for help.

We can't even help ourselves, thought Jaller, as he doubled over in pain. *If the mask is doing this to us . . . why? Why would it ask for our help and attack us at the same time?*

Then — as suddenly as it had begun — it was over.

The light was gone, along with the waves of energy. The incredible pain had ceased. The Toa floated in the water, still and quiet. Any sea predator who had approached just then would have kept on going, for there would be no sport in hunting the dead.

"We're . . . alive?" muttered Kalmah. "What an . . . unexpected surprise."

The tentacled being rose unsteadily to his feet. In his lifetime, Kalmah had been a conqueror, a ruler, and a prisoner. Most recently, his existence had been spent as a monstrous resident of the ocean's depths. Never before had he experienced anything like what had just happened.

Even now, it was hard to recall the events and still keep his fragile hold on sanity. He and his fellow warlords, the Barraki, had journeyed to a network of undersea caverns in search of the fabled Mask of Life. They had found it, all right, along with a venom eel mysteriously grown to 300 feet in length and a Matoran determined to smash the mask to pieces. The eel found better things to do and left, and the Barraki managed to stop the Matoran from carrying out his mission. But the second a Barraki laid hands on the mask, there was an explosion of light and energy that seared both eyes and minds.

How much time had passed since then, Kalmah did not know. He got to his feet, wrapping a tentacle around a rock to steady himself, and looked around. Two of his allies, Carapar and Mantax, were half-buried in the sand — no doubt they had crawled there, trying to get relief from the intense light. A third, Ehlek, was flat against a rock wall, babbling like a lunatic. But Pridak — where was Pridak?

The self-proclaimed leader of the Barraki, sharklike Pridak had been the one to grab the Mask of Life. It was right after he had proclaimed that he intended to use the mask against all of the Barraki's enemies that the blinding light had appeared all around. If that light came from the mask, then Pridak would have been the one closest to it. Kalmah had no great love for Pridak — he had, after all, lost an eye to "the Shark" long ago — but if anything had happened to him, it might have happened to the mask as well.

And we need that mask, he reminded himself. *With it, we can shed these freakish forms, breathe air once more, and escape this undersea Pit. Then we can be again what we once were: absolute rulers of vast empires, masters of every land we walk upon.*

The small tentacles on the back of Kalmah's head detected sudden movement. He whirled in the water to see the Onu-Matoran, the one who had tried to break the mask, swimming frantically away. For a moment, Kalmah considered grabbing the Matoran and squeezing until something cracked. Then he decided against it. After all, where could the little one go — back to his home city, Mahri Nui? There was no safety to be had there.

Kalmah probed the cave with his tentacle.

When nothing grabbed, bit, or burned the limb, he felt it was safe to go in. It didn't take long to find Pridak. The stark white Barraki was stretched out on the ground, a mask gripped fiercely in his claws. Kalmah could see a large crack running from the top edge of the mask all the way down one side.

"You're going to shatter it," he said, reaching down to pry the mask out of Pridak's hands.

Pridak flashed his sharp jaws and lashed out at Kalmah, landing a kick that would have pulverized a lesser being. "Stay away! It's mine!" he raged.

Kalmah backed away slowly. He could see the madness in Pridak's eyes. If someone didn't calm the white Barraki soon, the mask would wind up in pieces, along with all their hopes of escape.

Where's Takadox and his hypnotic gaze when I need him? Kalmah thought. *There's nothing wrong with Pridak that a good will-sapping wouldn't cure.*

On the other side of the undersea mountain, Takadox was just waking up. His memory of just how he had wound up lying in a trench on the seafloor was jumbled. But one glance upward took care of that.

Ah, yes, he said to himself. *The beast . . .*

Takadox had spotted the massive venom eel and thought to use his hypnotic powers to bring it under his control. The eel had other ideas, slamming into the Barraki and sending him tumbling down into the depths. It was sheer luck Takadox had not wound up a shattered pile of parts.

"This is what I get for leaving my comfortable cave and trying to do my own dirty work," he said to himself. "Next time, I will trance Carapar and he can play tag with that overgrown worm."

Takadox shook his head and glanced up. Six forms were floating in the water far above him. At first, they were so still he thought they must be dead. Then fire flashed from the hand of one of them. Takadox knew then who they had to be, and braced for an attack, thinking they might have seen him.

As it turned out, he didn't have to be

concerned. The six figures had not noticed the Barraki down below. No, they had been noticed themselves, by the huge creature that had felled Takadox moments before.

For the moment, Takadox forgot his mysterious quarry. He settled himself on a flat rock to watch six Toa get eaten by a venom eel the size of a small mountain.

Oh, this is going to be good, he thought. *Too bad there are no Matoran nearby — after all, what good is a show without snacks?*

Dekar wasn't ready to die.

He was swimming as quickly as he could for Mahri Nui, but knew he wasn't going to make it. The air bubble that surrounded him was a split second away from disappearing completely. He could hold his breath, but not long enough to reach another source of air. He was going to perish here, in the black waters beneath his village, with the knowledge that he might have doomed his friends.

The Mask of Life had fallen into his hands,

although he had not known then what it was. Just having it in his possession warped his existence, as he found himself unable to kill anything — even creatures threatening Mahri Nui. Every time he made a strike, the wound would heal instantly. Blaming the mask and believing it to be evil, he decided to destroy it. He took it to a sea cave and tried to smash it with a rock.

After that, things got a little unclear. He remembered a flash of energy and the appearance of a monstrous venom eel. Then five mysterious and dangerous beings calling themselves Barraki arrived, insisting he turn over the mask. When he refused, they attacked him and took it. There was an explosion of pure light, and the next thing he knew, the Barraki were scattered and he could escape.

Now it seemed certain the escape would fail. He would drown, his body slowly sinking to the ocean floor, and no one on Mahri Nui would know the danger they were in. The air bubble was completely gone now, only the breath in his lungs sustained him, and already he felt strange.

The world around him kept blinking in and out of existence. One moment, he was swimming for his life. The next, he was taller, more powerful, standing guard over imprisoned Barraki and other evil beings. Then reality returned and he was still so far from Mahri Nui and so close to the end.

Everything went dark . . . then painfully bright . . . then black again. *Is this what death feels like?* Dekar wondered. A name began to echo through his mind, one he had never heard before. *Hydraxon . . . Hydraxon . . .*

In the space of a heartlight's flash, he was dying . . . then already dead . . . and then reborn, full of life and strength. The crisis had passed. Now he knew he would not perish today.

But he was no longer Dekar. He was a black-armored being of power, a spirit of justice and vengeance, and his duty was clear. The Pit was a jail, all who lived there were prisoners, and he was here to slam the cell door shut.

Grimly, he turned toward Mahri Nui and began his journey again.

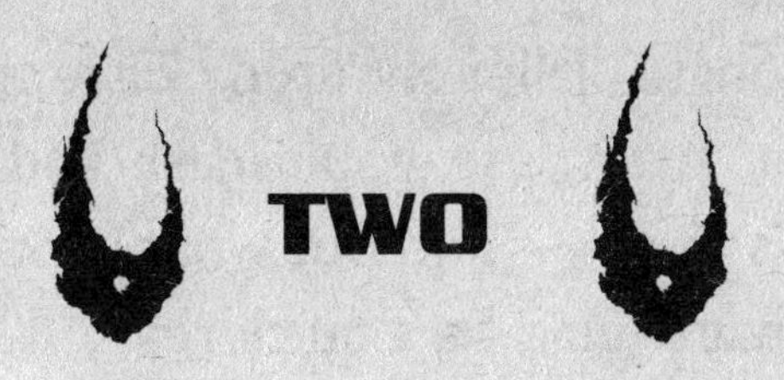

TWO

"Um, Kongu," said Hewkii. "We're underwater, right?"

"Yes," Kongu answered, sounding thoroughly disgusted. He had always hated the water.

"But we're breathing . . . and talking . . . and I haven't sunk to the bottom yet," said Hewkii. "Oh, and there's a giant eel heading right for us. This is another one of those illusions, right?"

Kongu looked down at himself. His armor was different, his weapons were gone, and he could feel a pair of tubes running from his back to the front of his mask. He felt different in other ways, too. The raw energy that had coursed through his body since he became a Toa was gone.

"Don't think so," answered Kongu. "No one's mad-twisted enough to conjure up anything this weird . . . or this wet."

"Kongu!" Jaller shouted. "Save the conversation for later. Use your mask and read that creature's mind — find out what it wants."

"That should be a quick read," Kongu muttered. He mentally triggered his Kanohi mask, all the while concentrating on the monstrous eel in front of him. As soon as he did it, he knew something was wrong. His Mask of Telepathy should have been reaching into the creature's mind and revealing whatever was there. But Kongu wasn't "hearing" any thoughts — instead he was suddenly surrounded by hundreds of smaller versions of the creature. One second, they hadn't been there, the next they were. He let out a yell of surprise and bolted away.

But the school of eels wasn't interested in Kongu or any of the other Toa. Instead, they were charging their larger cousin, mounting what had to be a doomed attack. Sure enough, the giant eel swallowed the lot of them in one gulp, then turned its attention back to the Toa.

Toa Matoro wasn't sure what good his mask power would be in this situation. After all, freeing his spirit from his body didn't add much in combat. At best, he could do a quick scout and find someplace the Toa could make a stand against this horror. He called on his mask power . . . and nothing happened . . . or, at least, nothing like what he had expected.

Down below, the long-dead hulk of a huge shark stirred. Its eyes opened and it began to swim stiffly toward the Toa and their monstrous foe. It wasn't alive again, not really, but the energy that made it move could be called an artificial spark of existence. While it didn't have the deadly grace of a Takea shark — moving more like a grotesque puppet — its teeth were still intact and sharp, as the giant eel found out when they sank into its side.

Matoro didn't waste time questioning. He summoned his elemental power, even knowing the lightning that was part of it might pose a risk to the other Toa in the water. But all that shot from his hands was ice — no energy. *This is impossible,* he thought. *I'm a Toa Inika! Our bodies are full of energy. . . . Where did it all go?*

The venom eel didn't care about any of that. It felt ice forming on its body, weighing it down, and it didn't like the sensation. It snapped its huge body like a whip, shattering the ice and hurling the shark away. Chunks of ice slammed into Matoro and Kongu. Jaller tried using his mask to dodge the chunks, only to find that he was suddenly hearing sounds bouncing off nearby objects.

This is bad, he thought. *Our weapons are gone, our masks have changed powers — and if we don't get a handle on what we can do now, we're going to be fish food.*

Something shot past him on the left side. It was Hahli, swimming at high speed around and around the eel and hurling bolts of electricity from her hands. Nuparu suddenly faded into view above the eel's head, calling on earth from the ocean floor to slam into the creature. Jaller decided to put off his questions until later, instead sending a rain of fire bolts at the beast.

All the Toa's efforts were managing to do was enrage the monster. At its size, their attacks felt like the stings of a trifle fish. It charged forward, slamming into the assembled heroes and scattering them. Hahli and Nuparu were left in its wake, but it was already turning to go after them. They were hardly big enough to make a meal out of, but at least once swallowed they would stop being such an annoyance.

The eel swam as swiftly as it could, anticipating the end of the hunt. Then its dim brain noticed that no matter how much it tried, it wasn't getting any closer to its prey. In fact, it was taking much more effort to move forward at all. Its body felt heavy, and was growing heavier by the moment. Now it couldn't swim at all anymore but only sink rapidly toward the bottom. It slammed into the ocean floor with an impact that rattled the surrounding undersea mountains, stunned into unconsciousness.

Mystified, Hahli watched the whole thing happen. Then she glanced up to see a smiling Hewkii swimming awkwardly toward her, pointing at his mask.

"This is more like it," he said. "Hey, a Toa of Stone ought to be able to make something sink like a rock, right?"

It was Nuparu, his eyes accustomed to seeing in the dark, who spotted the Matoran village resting on a plateau. There were no lights anywhere to be seen, but he could spot movement among the buildings. *Matoran?* he wondered. *How could they survive down here? Then again, how are we doing it?*

He was pretty sure he knew what his mask did now. Its effects matched the description of the Mask of Stealth once worn by Toa Nidhiki. He could fade into the background and make virtually no noise as he swam. It was perfect for scouting out the village.

It wasn't like any place Nuparu had ever seen. The buildings were surrounded by giant bubbles of air, and the Matoran swam inside of much smaller bubbles that conformed to the shape of their bodies. Right now, the mood in the underwater city was tense, with citizens manning strange weapons and waiting for an attack.

Nuparu decided that six Toa suddenly charging in wouldn't be a good idea. He backed well away from the border and turned off his mask power, allowing the Matoran to see him clearly.

Their reaction was immediate. Weapons opened fire, hurling spheres of solidified air at the Toa of Earth. One struck Nuparu and dissolved into a cloud of pure air. He choked as the gas entered his lungs. More shots followed as the Matoran tried to drive him away. He couldn't catch his breath long enough to tell them who he was and that he meant no harm.

A jet of super-hot flame came down from above, striking the launcher and melting it into slag. Nuparu looked up to see Jaller and the others swimming toward him. The Matoran saw them, too, and fled, but not in panic. Instead, they got their hands on another launcher and began dragging it back toward their post.

"Hold it!" Jaller shouted. "We're not here to fight you!"

"Got a funny way of showing it," one Po-Matoran shot back, pointing at the ruined launcher. "We know what you Pit types are like — bunch of liars and murderers. Well, you're not getting into Mahri Nui!"

"Pit? Mahri Nui? What are you talking about?" asked Hahli. "We were told there was a Matoran village down here that needed saving, and —"

"We can save ourselves," said the Po-Matoran. "Next thing, you'll be telling me you're not from the Pit — that you're Toa, or some black water like that."

"We are Toa," said Nuparu.

"Yeah," added Kongu. "Who else dresses like this?"

"Then where were you?" the Po-Matoran asked, pain and anger in his voice. "Where were you when Mahri Nui sank? Where have you been all this time, when Barraki were picking us off one by one for the fun of it?"

"Enough." The command came from a Le-Matoran who had approached from the village. He put a hand on the Po-Matoran's shoulder and then nodded to two others. They came and gently led the villager away. Once he was gone, the Le-Matoran looked at the Toa. "My name is Defilak. I am the leader of Mahri Nui's council for this span-time. What do you want here?"

"I am Toa Matoro," said the Toa of Ice. "We came to your village seeking a mask that has been lost. It is vital that we recover it."

Defilak frowned. "You are the second being to ask me about a mask in the last day. The first followed up his question by killing one of my friends, just to show-scan that he could do it."

"I'm . . . sorry," said Matoro.

"One of you may enter the village," Defilak said. "The rest of you — if you really are heroes — defend Mahri Nui. The fields of air are held hostage by ever-dangerous Rahi. Free them, and perhaps my people will see you for what you speak-say you are."

Matoro swam forward, passing through the skin of an air bubble as he followed Defilak. Immediately, he faltered. He couldn't breathe!

Hearing his gasps, Defilak turned around and shoved him roughly back out of the bubble. After a few moments, Matoro found he was all right again.

"I don't understand," said the Toa of Ice. "What just happened?"

"How can you not know?" asked Defilak. "You are a creature of the sea, Matoro. You must have known you can't breathe air."

Matoro, shocked, didn't answer. All he could think of was the words "can't breathe air"— if that was the case, how could he and the others ever return to Metru Nui, their home? Had the search for the Mask of Life doomed them to life under the sea?

"This shouldn't be too difficult," Toa Hahli said, pointing to the vast fields of air. At first, it had seemed as if the strange plants were moving. A closer look revealed that nasty-looking Rahi crabs were everywhere in the fields, easily fighting off Matoran attempts to dislodge them.

"Five of us, five thousand of them," said

Kongu. "I like your idea of fair odds. And what's with the fins?"

"What?"

"You have fins. They look kind of like wings. And a big claw."

"Have you looked at yourself lately?" asked Hahli. "Or any of the others? We've all changed."

"I dodged the fins thing, though."

"The Mask of Life," said Jaller. "I . . . heard it . . . felt it . . . when we entered the water. It must have done this to us so we could survive down here."

"Then it's officially off my Naming Day gift list," grumbled Kongu.

"The one thing I hoped we might get out of being underwater is that Kongu wouldn't be able to talk," said Hewkii. "Come on, we have a job to do."

"Um, maybe we don't. Look," said Nuparu, pointing to the fields.

Jaller had to summon his flame to provide enough light for the Toa to see. What the glow revealed was the amazing sight of thousands of keras crabs crawling out of the fields they had been infesting. They weren't fleeing but backing slowly away from the stalks of airweed, then stopping about twenty yards from the fields. The crabs stood right on the edge of the landmass, their backs to the black water. Then they were joined by other creatures — sharks, squid, venom eels, rays, and other Rahi of the deep. The beasts made no threatening moves, just hovered in the water, silently regarding the Toa.

"Okay, Hahli, you're the one with water on the brain," said Hewkii. "Do sea Rahi like this normally act this way, or is it what it looks like — really creepy?"

"No, it's not normal," Hahli replied. "This is weird . . .'Makuta comes up and gives you a hug' weird. It's almost like they're . . . waiting for something . . . or someone."

"And so they are."

The Toa turned as one. Floating before them were six strange beings, shaped vaguely like Toa but with mutations that made them look like bizarre sea monsters. Behind them were gathered more killers of this underwater world, tails slashing the water, tentacles eager to squeeze fresh prey.

"And people wonder why I hate the water," said Kongu.

THREE

One of the six swam a little way forward and peered at the Toa. He was slightly bent, with small, piercing eyes and mandibles that snapped open and shut repulsively. "Ah, me, what have we here?" he rasped. "Five little Toa who have lost their way? We would have been here sooner to greet you, but you know, it's never wise to go swimming too soon after a meal."

A larger brute with two crablike claws spoke up next. "I don't like it. What are they doing here now? Something smells."

"That would be you, Carapar," said the first. "Comes from eating those six-foot-long blood snails . . ."

"Quiet," said a white being, this one resembling a Toa-size shark. At first, the heroes thought he might have lost an arm in combat. Then they realized he was just keeping one hand behind his back. "I am Pridak. We are the Barraki, and this is our realm. Tell us why you are here, and perhaps you will live to see another tide."

The bent being leaned forward and whispered conspiratorially. "Better listen to Takadox, masked ones. Pridak was . . . not himself . . . or rather, too much himself, a little while ago. I did a little trick of mine to calm him down — otherwise, he might kill you first and then ask questions of your corpses. This way works much better, you see."

"Answer," said Pridak. "What did you do to be exiled here?"

"Exiled?" said Hewkii. "We're not —"

"— In the habit of explaining ourselves to every bait fish that comes along," Hahli interrupted. "By what right do you and your pathetic schools of minnows interfere with us?"

Kalmah surged forward. "By right of conquest!" he said, reaching with his tentacle to try and grab Hahli. The Toa of Water grabbed the appendage and yanked hard, hauling Kalmah off his feet and hurtling through the water toward her. He slammed face-first into her open hand and dropped to the ocean floor, sputtering and cursing. She cast his tentacle aside like it was a piece of flotsam that had drifted by.

"Do you have any other answer to give?" said Hahli. "Or are you content to tread water and bluster like toothless Takea sharks?"

"You have heard of the Barraki before?" asked Pridak.

"Yes," said Hahli. "Their name has come down the millennia . . . a relic used to frighten pathetic Matoran and keep them in their beds at night."

The other Barraki looked at Pridak, fully expecting him to fly into a rage and rend this insolent Toa. Instead, he smiled, revealing row upon row of daggerlike teeth. "Perhaps," he said. "Our day was long ago. But a new era is about to begin . . . and it starts with this."

Pridak brought his hand from behind his back. The Toa couldn't help but gasp, for in his claw he held the Mask of Life. "You recognize it?" he said. "Interesting. So few have seen this mask and lived."

"I do," said Hahli. "And I have. Aren't you worried about its legendary curse?"

"Curse?" Pridak repeated. Then he roared, "Look at me . . . look at where I dwell . . . look at my companions, once rulers, now monstrosities, and tell me — how much more cursed could we be?"

"Relax, Pridak," said Takadox. "Stay in control."

"I thought you said there were six of them," Carapar said to Takadox. "I only count five."

"It counts?" said Hahli, in mock surprise. "Amazing. To answer your dull-witted question, we *were* six — but profits go farther shared among five, if you catch my current."

"Bring them along," said Pridak. "We have a long journey ahead of us, and disgraced Toa might prove useful."

"As allies?" whispered Kalmah.

Pridak shook his head. "It's always best,

when traveling, to make sure you bring lunch along."

Kalmah, Carapar, and a third, spindly being covered with sharp spines, moved behind the Toa. Pridak, Takadox, and their other companion, Mantax, turned and began to swim away. The unspoken intention was that the Toa follow behind, which they did, flanked by armies of sea creatures.

Jaller turned to Hahli and said softly, "So. When did you become 'Hahli the Barbarian'?"

"Trust me, I know what I'm doing," the Toa of Water answered. Then she smiled, adding, "Besides, it's sort of fun."

Matoro stood just outside one of the large air bubbles that dotted Mahri Nui. Defilak stood on the other side of the bubble's skin, flanked by two armed Ta-Matoran.

"This has been a disastrous day," Defilak said quietly. "Dekar is missing . . . Sarda is dead . . . and who knows how many other Matoran heroes were injured."

"I'm sorry," said Matoro. "I wish we had gotten here sooner. But time is running out and we need that mask."

"Mask! Mask!" Defilak snapped. "There is no mask! I have never heard of any —"

"The fields of air are free again!" The shout came from Idris, a Ga-Matoran. She swam up to Defilak, barely able to contain her excitement. "The keras crabs have withdrawn. We can harvest the air again!"

Toa Matoro smiled. His friends had done their job and proven that they were true heroes. Now they could get on to the vital work of reclaiming the Mask of Life. "I told you," he said. "I knew the others wouldn't let you down."

"The others?" said Idris, puzzled. "Do you mean the five who look like you? I saw them talking with the Barraki, and then they left with them."

"They're prisoners?" asked Matoro.

"No," said Idris. "Looked more like partners to me."

Defilak turned to Matoro, suspicion in his

eyes. The Toa realized he would have to make a break for it, no matter how bad it looked, and go find the others. Something strange was going on down here and he had to find out what.

Before the Matoran could train their solid-air launchers on him, Matoro turned the water in front of them to ice. Then he wheeled around and swam for the fields of air. He had gone only a few yards when something flew past him and exploded. The shock wave sent him tumbling through the water, head ringing.

When Matoro finally came to a stop, he was lying at the feet of a figure in pitch-black armor. He was armed with wicked blades and a multishot blaster, and he regarded Matoro as if the Toa were something he had just stepped in.

"Welcome to the Pit, runner," the figure said. "My name is Hydraxon. You have the right to remain jailed."

The five Toa had been escorted back to a desolate area, and each was invited to occupy a sea cave. Although Pridak insisted they were "guests," the sharks and squid hovering outside the entrances made it very clear that they weren't meant to leave.

Nuparu waited until the Barraki had all departed. Then he triggered his mask power. He hoped that its power of stealth would be enough to let him escape.

Glancing down, Nuparu saw his hand had become almost ghostly in appearance. Anyone looking at him would barely see an outline of his form, and probably mistake it for a trick of the water. He slipped out of the cave entrance, attracting no notice from the giant squid on guard, and made his way to where Hahli was being held.

"Hahli!" he whispered. She took no notice. Nuparu swam behind her and turned off the mask, so he could return to full visibility. "Hahli!"

She turned, saw him, and jumped from her rock. "Nuparu!" she said, quietly but forcefully. "Makuta's bones, you scared ten thousand years off me! What are you doing here?"

"You told Jaller you knew something," said Nuparu. "I figured it was time for share and tell."

Hahli nodded. As quickly and quietly as she could, she recounted how Turaga Whenua had once toured her through the shattered remnants of the Metru Nui Archives. She had spent time rummaging among some old tablets, trying to decipher them. One particularly old carving told the story of the League of Six Kingdoms.

"At the height of their power, the six members of the League — Pridak, Takadox, Carapar, Ehlek, Mantax, and Kalmah — dominated most of the known universe. When they tried to combine their armies and rebel against the Great Spirit Mata Nui, they were crushed by the Brotherhood of Makuta. The records are sketchy after that, saying only that they were condemned for their crimes and taken away for punishment."

"Then what are they doing down here?"

"I don't know, but maybe . . . what if they were imprisoned somewhere . . . and when the Great Cataclysm struck our home, it hit other places, too? A massive earthquake could have shattered their cells and set them free. But, mutated as they are now, they can't reclaim their kingdoms . . . unless somehow the power of the Mask of Life can make them what they once were."

Nuparu didn't need to hear anymore. "Our only advantage is they think we're as bad as they are and were condemned here as well. We need to break out and get the mask before they can use it."

"It's worse than that," said Hahli. "I overheard Takadox and Kalmah talking. The mask is cracking and crumbling; its power is leaking out. If we don't act soon . . . there won't be any Mask of Life left to save."

Matoro was thrown roughly into a cave. A barred door was slammed shut behind him.

"You could probably break out of here, runner, if you really wanted to," said Hydraxon. "Let me show you why you don't want to."

The armored figure beckoned to someone

out of sight. A few moments later, a powerful-looking crimson mechanoid stepped into view. And a vicious, wolflike Rahi strained against the leash it held.

"This is Maxilos," said Hydraxon. "Being completely mechanical, he is the perfect guard, for he cannot be bribed or deceived. His reflexes are faster than any living being. Watch."

Hydraxon picked up a rock and hurled it into Matoro's cell. It had barely passed through the bars before Maxilos fired an electric bolt from its sword, shattering the rock to dust.

"The pet is Spinax," Hydraxon continued. "Once it has your scent, it will follow you to the edge of the universe and beyond for however many centuries it takes. So I suggest you make yourself comfortable, runner. You're going to be here a long time."

Matoro watched Hydraxon go, leaving Maxilos behind to guard him. He began calculating the odds. Since Maxilos wasn't a living being, he wouldn't have to hold back. A few quick ice darts into the mechanoid's inner workings would take care of it, and some ice chains would hold the Rahi for a while.

He readied himself. Maxilos was standing completely still, just staring at Matoro. Then, apparently satisfied the Toa was no threat, the mechanoid turned its back.

Now! thought Matoro. He took aim, prepared to hurl ice at his guard. But then he suddenly grew confused. What was he doing here? How could he trigger his powers? His body felt weak and slow and all he wanted to do was sleep. His mind was awhirl with emotions, rage one moment, fear the next.

Maxilos turned around, but the mechanoid was very different from how it had been a moment before. Gone was the blank expression of a purely mechanical being, replaced by a sinister smile that was all too familiar.

"We meet again, Matoro," said Maxilos. "The last time, our positions were reversed. . . . I was the vanquished, while you stood with the victors. But you were always wiser than Jaller, Hewkii, and the rest of those spineless, self-important fools. You knew I wasn't gone for good."

Matoro felt colder than any ice could ever be. "You can't be here . . ." he breathed.

"And why not? This is a perfectly good, if stiff and ungainly, body. And you must admit, it is better than life as a green and black cloud stuffed inside a crystal vat."

"Makuta . . ." Matoro could still hardly believe it. He knew all too well the master of shadows had survived repeated brushes with destruction, but it was still horrifying to come mask to mask with him again. "Are you here to kill me, then?"

"Call me Maxilos," was the reply. "Everyone else here does. I prefer to keep my true identity to myself for now. As for your question . . . kill you, Matoro? No, I'm here to free you. But first . . ."

The right arm of Maxilos pointed at Matoro. The next instant, the Toa of Ice was rocked by a sonic blast, bolts of chain lightning, and shattering force. Any lesser being would have been dead three times over, but Matoro still lived . . . even if he wasn't very happy about it at the moment.

"Now we understand each other," said Maxilos/Makuta. "I'm on your side in this, Matoro. You would be wise to see that I stay there."

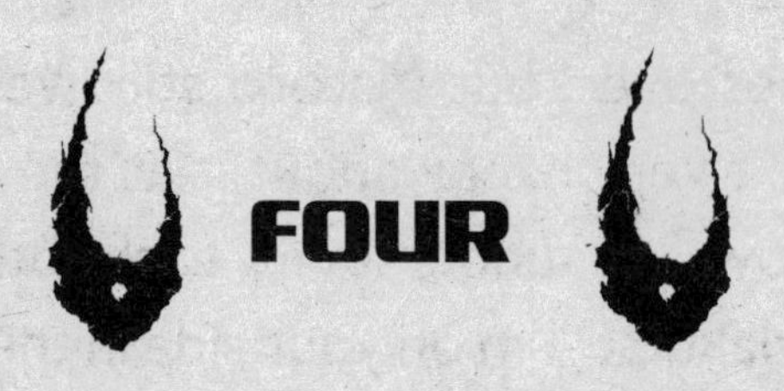

FOUR

Pridak slammed the Mask of Life down on a stone pedestal. "Today, the reign of the Barraki begins again," he announced. "With this mask, we can reclaim our empire."

The other five Barraki were assembled in the huge sea cave which served as Pridak's base. There were no cheers at his statement or vows of revenge on the world beyond the Pit. All five were rulers, veterans of a thousand campaigns, and not easily swayed by words. Nor did the sight of their sharklike ally and a crumbling Kanohi mask fill them with confidence.

Carapar was the first to speak. "How? Our old kingdoms are a long way away, Pridak, and on dry land — in case you hadn't noticed, none of us are exactly built for the surface world anymore."

In answer, Pridak snatched a tiny trill fish

out of the water and held it up to one of the cracks in the mask. Before the Barraki's startled eyes, the fish began to grow and mutate into something out of a Ga-Matoran's nightmare. When it was almost too large to hold, Pridak squeezed hard and crushed the unfortunate creature to death.

"You have all the imagination of a lump of coral, Carapar," said Pridak. "The mask is damaged, and its power is leaking out. All we have to do is wait for it to shatter and then bathe in its energies. We will be restored to what we once were, and the League of Six Kingdoms will live once more."

"And in the meantime?" said Mantax, his cold blue eyes locked onto Pridak. "Where will we keep the mask?"

"Here," Pridak replied.

A wave of unease passed through the Barraki. Pridak considered himself their leader, and they let him have that role rather than risk what his savage jaws could do to them. But if this mask was as powerful as he said, none felt comfortable with any one of them having it in his exclusive possession.

"How do we know you won't change yourself and leave the rest of us as we are?" Ehlek muttered. Kalmah took a step away from the eel-like Barraki. He could smell ozone in the water, a sign that Ehlek was gathering electrical energy.

"How dare you suggest —?" Pridak said, charging forward. Ehlek turned, unleashing a blast of electricity from his spines. The voltage caught Pridak dead-on, sending his body into spasms.

Takadox stepped in between the two. "Stop it! We won't get anywhere fighting over the mask. I say we put it in the Razor Whale's Teeth."

Pridak had regained control of his form. Kalmah and Carapar moved quickly to restrain him from tearing Ehlek apart. "Takadox is right," said Kalmah. "We shared our victories . . . and we shared our punishment. So we will share this mask, too, until we see if it can do all you claim."

"All right," Pridak said, shrugging off the

grip of the two Barraki. "I will take it there myself."

"We'll *all* take it there," said Ehlek.

"All but me," said Kalmah. "I am going to check on those Toa. Condemned to the Pit they may have been, but that doesn't mean they can be trusted. I would sleep better if they were food for the sea squid."

Takadox snatched the mask up in his claw and the Barraki went their separate ways, four heading for the depths of the Pit, while Kalmah and Carapar swam for the sea caves. None of them felt the eyes of Hydraxon upon them, or even dreamt that their long-dead jailer lived again. But he was there, watching their every movement, noting exactly what type of weapon would be needed to bring each one down.

By the time they were gone, his scouting mission was done. Now it was time for the hunt.

The Razor Whale's Teeth was a nickname given by the Barraki to a collection of triangular, dangerously sharp stones that jutted out of the ocean floor in a roughly circular pattern. The area was a favorite hunting ground of razor whales and their smaller cousins, the razorfish. The presence of amphibious proto drakes in the area served to keep Takea sharks away, as the drakes were one of the few sea creatures that fed on sharks.

The Barraki were still several yards away from the rocks when they spotted the presence of something else as well. A hulking, tentacled creature had made a camp right in the middle of the "teeth" and was busily devouring a giant squid. He had four arms, bulbous red eyes, and a spiked head that glowed in the dark waters. His frame was lean, but all muscle, and the sharp blades he carried were keen enough to slice through the tough hide of his dinner.

His identity was known, of course. He was a fellow escapee from the Pit named Nocturn, famous for being one of the few to be immune to the effects of the black water. Nocturn had not been mutated into what the Barraki saw before them — he had always been that ugly. In his calmer and more lucid moments, he served Ehlek well as a lieutenant. This was not one of those moments.

"Not that lummox," muttered Mantax. "Leave the mask here and he will probably eat it. Why is he in the Pit in the first place?"

"He was exiled from his home island after he broke something," said Takadox.

"What did he break?"

"The island." Seeing the doubt on Mantax's features, Takadox continued, "He was in a bad mood, the island wasn't very big, and he hit it in just the right spot . . . shows what lots of sleep, clean living, and razor whales for breakfast every day will do for you."

Pridak swam toward the rock formation, mask in one hand and one of Kalmah's squid launchers in the other. As soon as he spotted the Barraki, Nocturn sprang up and began slashing the water with his blades. "My place! Go away!" he bellowed.

"No one wants to take your place," said

Pridak. "We brought you a pretty mask to keep. You stay here and keep it safe. Understand? If someone other than us comes for it . . . consider them a free meal."

Nocturn took the Mask of Life and the launcher and looked from one to the other. He didn't seem particularly interested in either one.

"Do you know who I am?" asked Pridak.

Nocturn nodded. "Pridak. The Shark."

"Then you know what will happen if you don't do what I ask?"

Nocturn winced. He still bore the scars of an earlier run-in with Pridak, which had cost him one of his arms. Fortunately, it had grown back, though minus its tentacle. "Rip, slash," he said. "Pain. Hiding."

"And next time, I won't stop with your arm," Pridak said darkly.

Toa Nuparu found getting out of Hahli's cave to be just as easy as getting in had been. But the Toa of Water would not be able to just swim past the giant squid guarding her. She had told Nuparu he had no reason to worry. "It took some practice, but I finally know what this mask can do," she assured him. "When you get out of the cave, don't look my way, no matter what."

Nuparu knew better than to argue with her. She was, after all, the Toa with the best knowledge of the sea. He obligingly turned away once he was clear of the cavern. Had he not done so, he would have seen Hahli standing completely still at the mouth of the cave. The squid noticed her and began to move toward her, reaching out with its powerful tentacles. Then it paused. Bands of color were traveling up and down Hahli's body, shifting in intensity even as they moved faster. Puzzled, the squid watched intently, its huge eyes drawn to the bright colors and the pattern of their movement. In a matter of moments, the great sea beast was entranced.

The bands of color stopped moving and faded away. The squid did not react. Satisfied, Hahli swam right past it and joined Nuparu. "What happened?" asked the Toa of Earth.

"The mask," Hahli answered. "It lets me

mimic the powers of any sea creature. I remembered there was a hypnotic Rahi fish who could entrance prey, so I summoned that ability. The giant squid is unharmed, but when it awakens, we will be long gone."

"Sounds good to me," said Toa Hewkii, swimming toward them. "The problem with water is it's so . . . wet."

"How did you get past your guard?"

"I didn't. Used my mask to cut off his gravity," said Hewkii. "Too bad you missed it. You would believe a Takea shark can fly."

"Use your mask!" said Jaller.

Toa Kongu shook his head. "I'd really rather not."

Jaller floated in the water, feeling frustrated and helpless. His fire power had been enough to frighten off the venom eels that were guarding him, but the strain of using his elemental abilities underwater had exhausted him. On land, he was one of the most powerful Toa, but here he felt like one of the weakest. The best he could manage was a low, lukewarm flame from his sword, and that would not be enough to drive away the stingrays guarding Kongu.

He turned at a sound behind him. A large hahnah crab was scuttling toward him, apparently attracted by his fire. This far beneath the sea, heat and light were a rarity. Unlike most creatures, this one did not seem to fear the flames. It regarded the Toa of Fire curiously. Jaller wondered if he himself had worn the same expression when he was a Matoran villager, meeting Toa Tahu for the first time.

There wasn't time to worry about that now. Kongu had unleashed an underwater cylone and scattered the rays and was now heading for Jaller. By the time the two Toa heard the sound of a Barraki launcher being fired, it was too late. A slime-covered sea squid slammed into Kongu and latched itself onto his back with its tentacles. The Toa of Air struggled in vain to pull it free as the squid grafted itself onto his body. Once fully in place, the squid began draining the Toa's life energies. Kongu spasmed and sank toward the sea floor.

Toa Jaller raced to his aid, only to hear the launcher fire once more. He saw another squid hurtling toward him out of the darkness. He raised his sword and threw all his power into it, unleashing a blast of flame that incinerated the creature. There was no time to celebrate his victory. Two massive claws grabbed him from behind. Carapar lifted Jaller into the air and slammed him down hard onto the sea floor. Jaller rolled, scissored his legs onto the Barraki's and knocked his foe off balance.

A tentacle suddenly wrapped around the Toa's throat. It was Kalmah pulling Jaller toward him. Carapar regained his balance and grabbed Jaller's legs, one in each claw. "Time to make a wish," the crablike Barraki said.

Kongu could see all that was happening, but could not even help himself. Even concentrated air power could not tear the squid loose. With each moment, he was growing weaker.

Once he passed out, both he and Jaller would be doomed.

Something struck him. Kongu managed to turn his head to see the hahnah crab, which was now attacking the squid. Unable to fight back with its tentacles stuck to Kongu, the squid was being torn apart by the crab's claws. Mortally wounded, the squid finally released its hold and floated up toward the surface. Kongu felt his strength returning, but it wasn't fast enough. He had no choice — he had to use the power of his mask.

Closing his eyes tightly, he triggered his Kanohi mask. His few attempts at using it before had convinced him its power was to summon creatures to Kongu's side. But so far, each thing summoned had been worse or more bizarre than the last. He really didn't want to see what was coming next.

As it turned out, shutting his eyes didn't make things any better. He could feel the pounding beneath his feet, as if something was burrowing its way up from beneath the ocean floor. He could hear the sound of the ground being torn asunder nearby, the startled curses of the Barraki, and the panicked screech of the hahnah crab. Then he was tumbling through the water, struck by a massive undersea wave.

When he finally righted himself, Kongu opened his eyes. The first thing he saw was a grotesque sea creature, easily two hundred feet high, looking like a cross between a whale and the giant, clawed slime-worms Onu-Matoran miners had run into in the past. It was nothing that had ever lumbered through the seas of Metru Nui or anywhere Matoran dwelled. The creature was ancient when the world was new, a relic of a past age when it was probably dwarfed by its fellow creatures. It had slumbered for millennia until awakened by Kongu's Mask of Summoning . . . and it woke up in a bad mood.

At first, the Barraki were too stunned to know how to react. Then Kalmah snapped his tentacle, sending Jaller flying toward the beast. Kongu took off after the Toa of Fire, swimming as fast as he could. With both Toa occupied, the two Barraki vanished into the black water.

The creature caught sight of Jaller just before the Toa was going to strike its body. It lashed out with a clawed appendage and batted the Toa away, sending him back toward the ocean floor. He slammed into the approaching Kongu and both hit the earth hard.

"What . . . what is that?" asked Jaller. "Where did it come from?"

"Well, I told you I didn't want to use the mask," Kongu replied.

FIVE

Toa Nuparu had discovered a little corner of paradise beneath the sea. He, Hewkii, and Hahli had split up to search for the Mask of Life. Nuparu had found no sign of that, but he had stumbled upon a cavern full of treasures. When Hahli and Hewkii found him, he was busily testing out a multibarreled weapon that looked like something that would be mounted on an airship.

"Nuparu, what are you doing?" Hewkii demanded.

The Toa of Earth turned, startled, and accidentally hit the weapon control. A minirocket blasted from the launcher, hitting the cave wall right next to Hewkii and blowing a hole in it. The Toa of Stone barely got out of the way in time.

"Um, sorry," said Nuparu. "You shouldn't sneak up on people like that."

"Says the Toa wearing a Mask of Stealth," Hewkii grumbled. "What is all this? Planning to start a war?"

"No," said Nuparu. "Just planning to still be around when it's over."

The three Toa ran into Jaller and Kongu on the way back to Mahri Nui. None of them had seen any sign of the mask or had spotted Barraki during their search. But a large Takea shark with a damaged dorsal fin had been shadowing them since they reunited. The hahnah crab that was still following along behind Jaller bristled at the sight of the predator.

Nuparu and Hewkii had brought a load of the weapons from the cave. The inscriptions on the side of them read "Cordak revolving blaster." No one had a clue who had made them, but since "cordak" was a Matoran word meaning "desolation," it wasn't hard to guess their intended use. Kongu immediately took two. When the others gave him questioning looks, he simply said, "Two hands."

They expected to find Matoro waiting for them in Mahri Nui. Instead, they were met by a hail of solidified air bubbles from the city's defenses. Defilak stood by the launchers, saying, "Turn back! We have no need for ever-friends of the Barraki here!"

"All right," Jaller said to the others. "We don't have time for this. Hewkii, you and I will take out the launchers, and the rest of you —"

"I know an easier way," Hahli cut in. "Kongu, use your power — make the air inside that bubble shove him out of it."

"What good will that do?" asked Kongu. "He has a personal air bubble around him, so he can breathe in the water. He'll just swim back into the city."

Hahli smiled. "Oh, no, he won't. Do it."

Kongu summoned his elemental control of air, creating a hurricane force wind inside the air bubble directed just at Defilak. Before the Le-Matoran could grab on to anything, he had been flung out of the protective bubble and into the ocean. Hahli shot forward and began swimming in a circle around the Matoran, faster and faster, until the force of the whirlpool had stripped his air bubble away. All Defilak had left was the air in his lungs, and even that would not last long in the vacuum Hahli was creating.

Then the world abruptly stopped spinning. A strong arm grabbed him and hurled him back inside the city's protective bubble. It belonged to Hahli, who now hovered in front of the launchers as if daring the villagers to shoot. "You see? If I wanted you dead, you would be dead. I don't. Neither do my friends. We'd like to help, if you would just stop shooting at us long enough to let us do it."

"Why should I faith-trust you?" said Defilak. "Nothing in the Pit can be trusted."

"I am not of the Pit," said Hahli. "I am of the sea — it belongs to me, not to the Barraki or their servants. And through me, the sea belongs to you, too."

Defilak looked into the eyes of the Toa of Water. The decision he was about to make would change the future of Mahri Nui, for good or ill.

"Very well. We will lower our weapons . . . for now. But how will you help us?"

"The Barraki have something that belongs to us," said Jaller. "We are going to get it back."

"And they're going to resist . . . which is just too bad for them," said Hewkii. "Give us a hand, and maybe you'll have six less Barraki to worry about when it's all over."

When Hahli spoke again, it was more gently, as she remembered the valiant Matoran of Voya Nui. "Once that's done . . . there are some other friends you might want to meet. I know they will want to meet you."

"If you are what you say you are, we have much to talk-discuss," Defilak said. "But first, we will need to seek-find your other companion. He quick-fled into the black water and never returned . . . but with luck, maybe there is still a body left to recover."

Hovering in the shadowed waters nearby, Maxilos/Makuta smiled at his Toa companion.

"How sweet, Matoro," he said. "They are willing to spare a moment to recover your corpse."

"Shut up."

"Perhaps we should swim over there and tell them reports of your death are . . . premature. But not a word about who inhabits this crimson shell — you know what I can do to your friends, if I so choose."

Matoro looked into the dead eyes of the robotic Maxilos. It was hard to believe a being of ultimate evil hid inside that crude mechanical body. "Why? Why are you doing this to me?"

"Isn't it obvious? It's because you're so good at keeping secrets."

Far below, Nocturn had finally grown tired of staring at, handling, and tossing and catching the strange mask the Barraki had left with him. He could tell from the activity in the water around him that Ehlek and the other Barraki were planning something. Sharks and eels and squid and rays were darting every which way, getting themselves ready for action. He wished he was with them, tearing and rending and destroying enemies — always a cure for boredom.

Frustrated, he tossed the mask aside. It landed in the center of the Razor Whale's Teeth and settled into the soft sand. Nocturn reached out to grab a passing mudfish, looking forward to the sound it made when crushed. To his disappointment, the second he touched it, the fish died.

Puzzled, he tried again, only to find the same result. At first, it was sort of exciting. After all, he was now assured an endless supply of easily caught food. But somehow it was less satisfying when they didn't put up a fight, when the life just drained out of them in an instant.

So engrossed was Nocturn in his newfound ability that he stopped paying attention to the mask. He never noticed when a tiny blue sea creature crawled underneath the Mask of Life seeking shelter. Nor did he see the flare of energy from the mask when the little organism, called a gadunka, brushed against it. By the time he turned back to the mask, the damage was done.

Nocturn wasn't sure whether to be angry, pleased, or fearful about this new death touch he had acquired. He decided it would be best to go ask Ehlek about it. And if he ran into Pridak on the way . . . maybe Nocturn would shake his hand.

He picked up the Mask of Life and left in search of the Barraki. Behind him, the little gadunka was already beginning to grow.

The five Toa enjoyed a brief, if happy, reunion with Matoro. If they were curious about his chilly attitude when introducing their new ally, Maxilos, they didn't comment on it. There wasn't time to worry about the Toa of Ice's moods, not with the Mask of Life to find and an entire ocean to search.

It was Maxilos who suggested the Toa would be better served by splitting up. Matoro started to object, then apparently thought better of the idea. Feeling it would be best that no one travel alone, Jaller suggested he would team with Kongu, Hewkii with Nuparu, and Hahli with Matoro and Maxilos.

"That's all right," the Toa of Water said. "I will move faster on my own. After all, I'm more at home here than any of you."

As they double-checked their weapons, Defilak swam near. "Perhaps living so long in this night-black water has made us see only darkness in others," he said. "If you are truly about to face great trouble-danger on behalf of Mahri Nui . . . we would be honored to call you Toa Mahri."

Not so very long ago, the Toa Inika had been Matoran. They had met Toa who came to their island and placed their faith and trust in those heroes. Their faith had been rewarded. Now it was their turn to protect a village of Matoran who were relying upon them. It was Matoro who finally put what they were all feeling into words.

"The honor is ours, Defilak," he said. "We'll try to prove worthy of your trust."

Oh, yes, thought Makuta, master of shadows, in the body of Maxilos. *Indeed we will.*

SIX

Carapar looked back in time to see the horror dredged up from the sea floor locked in combat with the revived giant venom eel. It seemed like the sort of bad dream he usually had after feasting near Mantax's reef. The Pit had always been a grim, nasty, and thoroughly revolting place to live, but now it was becoming downright unhealthy.

He and Kalmah made for the latter's cave, passing the "squid farm" on the way. Carapar would never had admitted it, but he always found this place a bit disturbing. Kalmah had discovered the existence of the sea squid shortly after the Barraki's escape from imprisonment. They were unlike any creature the warlords were familiar with. For one thing, they had no armor or mechanical parts; they were purely organic tissue. For another, they did not come into being in a normal way, but rather were hatched from spheres with a thin, white surface.

Kalmah found the creatures intriguing, particularly their habit of draining the life force directly out of their prey. He began to breed them, taking care to starve and abuse the young squid so that they grew up vicious and ravenous. This made them the perfect living weapons. With some reluctance, he shared the use of them with the other Barraki, but no one was under any illusions about the creatures. If Kalmah ever moved against his fellow Barraki, the vampiric sea squid would be part of his legion.

As they entered the cavern, both Barraki were surprised to see the other warlords waiting for them. Takadox and Mantax were in darkened corners, feasting on any squid too slow or weak to escape from them. Ehlek was on the cave floor, in obvious pain from a bad gash on the organic tissue of his shoulder. Pridak stood over him, teeth bared.

"For the last time, Ehlek — where is he? Where has he taken the mask?"

Ehlek shook his head. "I don't know. Do you think I'm such a fool that I'd let Nocturn leave with the mask and not go with him?"

"I don't know," answered Pridak. "You are foolish enough to try my patience, so nothing is beyond your depths of idiocy."

"What is this?" demanded Kalmah. He used his tentacle to yank first Takadox, and then Mantax, out into the center of the cave. Takadox just smiled in response, a lone squid arm still dangling from his mandibles. Seeing Kalmah's gaze fixed on it, he said, "Snacks for later."

"We left the Mask of Life with Nocturn," said Mantax, in a tone that suggested no other explanation was necessary.

"And he's walked off with it," Kalmah guessed correctly. "Since he's Ehlek's lieutenant, Pridak decided an interrogation was needed . . . code for 'Pridak hadn't eaten in an hour.'"

"Actually, we thought perhaps you, Carapar,

and those Toa might have persuaded Nocturn to hand it over, and then . . . eased him out of this life," said Takadox. "But don't worry, Kalmah. I told them you would never do such a thing."

"Of course not," said Kalmah.

"For one thing, you're not that smart," Takadox finished.

"I don't have the mask, but I know where to look," Kalmah said, ignoring the jibe. "The Toa — they've escaped. They must have found it and taken it."

"Then we find them," snarled Pridak. "And when we're done, we scatter the remains to the sharks."

Kalmah hauled Ehlek to his feet and the Barraki exited the cave, Takadox and Mantax lagging behind. "Always to the sharks," said Takadox. "Ah, well, I almost feel sorry for that group of Toa, hunted and doomed as they are . . . and just when they thought it was safe to come into the Pit."

Toa Hahli swam slowly through a massive coral reef, her eyes scanning the ocean floor. She had used the power of her mask to give her perfect vision in the dark waters, so that the Mask of Life would not escape her sight. The result was a view of ocean life beyond anything she had ever imagined. The myriad creatures who swam in and around the reef looked nothing like the fish she had so often caught off the island of Mata Nui. Some were hideously ugly, others stunningly beautiful, and all strange and different in some way. If her mission were not so desperate, she could easily have spent days just exploring this natural wonder.

I wish Matoro or Jaller could see this, she thought. *They are both always so serious, especially Jaller. I wonder where it's written that Toa of Fire are not allowed to smile?*

A powerful pincer erupted out of the ground, grabbing her around the waist. Before she could react, she had been yanked down to the ocean floor hard enough to stun her. Hahli heard the sands shifting and the clicking of metallic mandibles. She swung her triple-bladed weapon blindly. It struck something hard and she heard a cry of pain. In that moment, the pincer's grip on her weakened slightly. She kicked free and turned to see her attacker.

Mantax was half in and half out of the sand. Her blow had struck him below his armored shoulder plates, damaging the muscle. He looked at Hahli with pure hatred and surged up toward her, trying to jab her with his head spikes. She dodged his thrust, then fired her cordak blaster at the sea bottom. The resulting explosion of sand blinded Mantax. He whirled this way, then that, but by the time he could see again, Hahli was gone.

The Barraki knew the Toa had not gone far. She was stalking him, as he was her. He made preparations, and then slipped back underground at the main junction of the reef. There he waited, his spikes and his blue eyes barely visible above the sand. Eventually, she would swim by again and he would have her.

Not very far away, Hahli was swimming slowly through the narrow passages of the reef. She had used her mask power to give her a chameleon ability, so that her body blended in with her surroundings. She knew the outcome of her skirmish with the Barraki was an exception to the rule. Under the sea, whoever struck first usually won the battle, and Hahli was determined it would be her.

There! She spotted Mantax's telltale spikes jutting out of the sand just ahead. The Barraki was keeping watch in the other direction. He would never see her attack coming until it was too late. Hahli struck, firing her blaster even as she unleashed her elemental water power.

Suddenly, something jabbed into the muscles of her right leg. She turned her head to see Mantax behind her, using his head spikes to inject paralyzing venom. Confused, she looked back and saw that her blast had unearthed a pile of sea creature bones, no doubt placed there by the Barraki as a decoy. Already, she could feel her limbs going numb as the venom spread. In a few moments, the paralysis would reach her lungs and she would die here, in the depths of the Pit.

* * *

Jaller waited for Kongu to say something. He could see that the Toa of Air was just itching to make a comment about being underwater and having to search cave after cave instead of being under an open sky and soaring on the wind.

"All right, say it," said the Toa of Fire.

"Say what?"

"You know what," said Jaller. "Some tree-speak complaint about being cold and wet, bumping your head on cave ceilings, and already being tired of smelling like fish . . . just say it and let's get it over with, so we can keep searching."

"No, I don't deep-think I will."

"Why not?"

"I don't have to," said Kongu. "You already speak-said it. By the way, is this cave number four hundred or five hundred? I lost count."

Jaller sighed. "Do you ever stop joking? You didn't act like this when you commanded the Gukko bird force in Le-Koro, did you?"

Kongu shrugged. "I wasn't one of six Toa deciding the fate of the universe then, either. Sure, I was grim and serious a lot of the time running the force — but Toa Lewa Nuva taught me that sometimes a little humor helps everyone relax and keep things in perspective. Besides, Jaller," he added, with a smile, "between you and Hewkii, 'grim and serious' is already covered on this team."

Jaller nodded. Not for the first time, he reminded himself that Kongu could have done just as good a job leading the team as he had. Matoro and Hahli, on the other hand, didn't have experience leading Matoran into battle. Yet somehow the Toa of Ice seemed to want to take charge, and Hahli had insisted on exploring on her own despite his warnings. *Before this crisis is over,* he thought, *this team is going to have to come together behind one leader — whether it's me or someone else.*

The two Toa swam into the cavern. Kongu did have another good point — they had been searching hours and found nothing, and it was beginning to look like the Barraki had found a better hiding place for the mask than a cave. But they wouldn't know until they had searched them all.

"Hey," said Kongu. "What are those?"

Jaller glanced to his right. The base of the cave wall was lined with white spheres. He moved closer for a better look. They weren't rocks or some kind of natural deposit. Their surface was smooth, but seemed fragile, and he was amazed none had broken, stacked on top of each other as they were. Jaller reached out to touch one and his eyes widened.

"There's something alive in there!" he said. "I can feel it moving!"

Kongu pointed back toward the cavern entrance. "There are more back there, and the shells are cracking. Do you think this is some kind of home-nest for really short Bohrok?"

"Or that thing that attacked you before . . . Be prepared for anything."

"Oh," said Kongu. "I could prepare a lot better from outside . . . way outside, even."

Before the startled eyes of the two Toa Mahri, the shells cracked. Tentacles of varying colors slithered between the cracks, forcing the openings wider. A cylindrical body and head appeared next, cold eyes regarding the Toa. Then the sea squid launched themselves at the heroes, hungry for their first meal. Dozens of the creatures swarmed over the two Toa, latching on with their tentacles and draining the life energies of their prey. Before Jaller or Kongu could defend themselves, they felt their strength deserting them.

Just before the world went black, Jaller looked up to see Kalmah and Carapar standing at the mouth of the cave. "Feed, my little ones," Kalmah said. "But leave something for your master as well."

"Can I ask you something?" said Nuparu to Hewkii. The two were making their way through a deep trench in the ocean floor, searching for some sign of the Mask of Life.

"What?"

"Do you ever miss home? I mean, Metru Nui?"

"Sure, I do," Hewkii shrugged. "Don't you?"

"All the time," said Nuparu. "I guess it's just . . . you were always so popular, you had a lot of friends. You have a lot to miss, but you don't talk about home very much."

Hewkii floated down to a rocky outcropping and looked at Nuparu. "Listen, just because I don't sit around complaining about how much I miss my home and my friends, that doesn't mean I don't think about them. But we have a job to do, Nuparu, and I figure the sooner we get it done, the sooner I can see home again. Feeling sad about what I miss is a luxury I don't have time for right now."

"I understand," Nuparu said. "Hey, what's that?"

The Toa of Earth was pointing to a large mass in the center of the trench, just barely in their range of vision. As they moved closer, Hewkii saw it was a huge tree stump buried in the sand, roots up. The tangled roots sticking in all directions gave the stump the appearance of a large head with serpents for hair. It was only when they got right on top of it that the two Toa realized that in this case, appearances were not deceiving.

Nuparu's eyes, adjusted to seeing in darkness, spotted them first. "Eels!" he shouted.

Now Hewkii saw them. They were everywhere, their sleek, black bodies twisted around the roots. Sensing intruders, they slithered free and headed for the Toa.

"Oh, no, you're not," said Hewkii. Using his mask, he increased the pull of gravity on the nearest eels, slamming them into the ground. At the same time, Nuparu caused the sea floor to open, swallowing the eels' nest whole. Hewkii followed that up with a solid slab of stone that sealed off the opening. Startled, the rest of the creatures fled.

"Hahli would be proud," Nuparu chuckled. "Earth and stone, victors under the sea! Right, Hewkii?"

When he got no answer, Nuparu turned around. Hewkii was nowhere to be seen.

"Hewkii? Where are you?" the Toa of Earth said, activating his Mask of Stealth as he did so, not knowing it was already too late. His presence had been detected by a natural predator attuned to the movements of the water. Every move Nuparu made sent a tiny ripple through the ocean that pointed to his location.

He was getting nervous. Nothing could take Hewkii without a fight, but there was no sign of the Toa of Stone. Blaster at the ready, Nuparu swam back the way they had come, searching for his friend.

He didn't see the huge metallic claw until it was too late. The instant after he was seized in its grip, a powerful electric shock jolted him into unconsciousness. Thus Nuparu was spared the unpleasant feeling of being carried to the edge of an undersea chasm and dumped in, drifting down to rest beside Hewkii. Their captor turned from the watery would-be grave and walked away, having already forgotten about the two Toa.

Back when Toa Matoro had been just another villager on the island of Mata Nui, he had sat down to discuss with Kopaka Nuva what life as a Toa was like. The Toa Nuva of Ice had listened politely to his questions, and then said, "Half of being a Toa, Matoro, is being prepared for the unexpected. The other half is being smart enough to know that you really can't ever prepare for that which you don't expect."

"Then what do you do?" Matoro had asked.

"You improvise, translator," Kopaka Nuva replied. "And you try not to let your enemies find out you're doing it."

The words of the Toa Nuva of Ice came back to Matoro as he hovered in the water beside Maxilos. They were confronted by more than two hundred Takea sharks and an assortment of other sea creatures so revolting he didn't even care to look at them. If ever there was a time for improvising, this was it.

"All right, here's what we do," he said to his "partner." But Maxilos did not respond, simply looked straight ahead with a cold, robotic stare. There was no sign of Makuta's presence inside the armored form. *Great*, thought Matoro. *When he's not wanted — which is virtually all the time — you can't get rid of him. When you do want him, he's back to being a puff of smoke someplace.*

Pridak suddenly appeared in the midst of the sharks, flanked by Takadox. The latter eyed Matoro as if the Toa were a potential meal, and then said, "Tell us, Toa — where is the Mask of Life?"

Matoro saw Pridak snarl at his fellow Barraki. He couldn't hear what was said, but he could guess. *They've lost the mask — probably think we took it,* he thought. *But just in case we didn't, Pridak didn't want us to know it was missing. Too late now.*

"Sorry, I never discuss such important matters in the middle of an aquarium," the Toa of Ice said. "Tell the sharks to take a walk — or a swim — and we can have a talk."

Pridak smiled. The sharks moved in closer, restless for the hunt. "Do you know where you are, Toa? This is a Takea shark hunting ground. The sea floor underneath you is littered with the bodies of creatures that weren't fast enough to get away. Do you think you're fast enough?"

"I don't have to be," Matoro answered. "Not as long as I'm strong enough to fight back."

Triggering his elemental power, he froze the water around Pridak and Takadox into a solid block. It sank like a stone out of sight. He was just about to congratulate himself on an easy victory when he heard an explosion from down below and saw shards of ice flying through the water. They were followed by Pridak and Takadox, still scraping super-cold ice fragments off their limbs.

"Is that the best you can do, Toa?" said Pridak.

"I don't know. Are you worthy of my best?"

The Toa of Ice called upon his Kanohi mask power, throwing more willpower into the act than he ever had before. Far below, long-dead sea creatures began to stir as artificial life flooded their bodies. Heavy-lidded eyes snapped open as limbs shook off the sleep of ages. One by one, the vanquished rose, vengeance in their hearts. Scattered groups began to swim toward Matoro, gathering behind him in an undead legion. Some looked almost as powerful and formidable as they had the day they died. Others had obviously suffered the tender mercies of the Takea shark. Together, they were enough to make even a Barraki hesitate.

Across the span of black water, two armies stared into each other's cold eyes — one living, one an imitation of life. Pridak's gaze was fixed on Toa Matoro, searching for some sign of weakness. He saw none.

"We appear to be evenly matched," said the Barraki finally.

"Not so," Matoro replied, flashing a cold smile as he gestured to his reanimated army. "My side has nothing left to lose."

SEVEN

Under normal circumstances, Mantax would have enjoyed watching Hahli struggle for her life. After all, what good was having the ability to paralyze your prey if you couldn't watch its last moments, as it sank to the sea bottom gasping for breath?

Unfortunately, he had no time for that pleasure now. The Mask of Life was still missing, and if the Toa didn't have it, he would have to face the possibility that one of the other Barraki had claimed it. Mantax hoped that was not the case. After thousands of years allied with them in the League of Six Kingdoms, and many thousands more as prisoners of the Pit, it would have been a shame if he and his army of rays had to lay waste to everything the others had built.

It wasn't here. He had retraced her route, checked every possible hiding place along the way, but without success. There was nothing left to do but return to the Toa's corpse and plan his next course of action. Maybe this water Toa had passed the mask on to one of her allies? He should have thought to ask her before killing her.

The next thing Mantax knew, he had been pulled off his feet and was flying headlong through the water. He came to an abrupt stop, slamming into a rock wall. Then he was being yanked the other way, only to crash into another slab of stone. The two blows were enough to scramble his senses, but not so much he couldn't make out the Toa he had defeated swimming toward him.

"Riptide," said Toa Hahli. "You really should watch out for those."

"Impossible," hissed Mantax. "Riptides only happen near the shore. We are nowhere near land."

"Nothing is impossible," said Hahli. "I learned the ways of water from Turaga Nokama and Toa Gali Nuva. The ocean shelters me, heals me . . . and obeys me."

Mantax felt another current taking hold of him. This time, he dug his pincer into the rock so he could not be moved. "Then speak, Toa. A Barraki knows when to fight and when to listen."

"Why did you attack me?"

"How did you survive?"

"There are beasts of the sea immune to any venom, and I am as well, if I choose," Hahli answered. She added a silent thanks to her Kanohi mask, whose ability to grant her the powers of various ocean creatures had saved her.

"I want the Mask of Life," said Mantax. "I thought you had it."

"And I thought *you* did," said Hahli. "While we're fighting, whoever does have it will be escaping with it."

"Your friends?"

"No," Hahli said, shaking her head. "Yours."

Mantax regarded her coldly. As a rule, he had no use for Toa. They were too conscience-bound to be ruthless, and always so quick to oppose the plans of their betters. But one thing about them he believed to be true: Toa were not liars. And if this water Toa was telling the truth . . .

"I have no friends," said Mantax. "Only enemies I haven't killed yet."

"Nuparu! Wake up!"

"Go away," muttered the Toa of Earth. "I don't want to go to work today. There's a spare Boxor vehicle over there, if you want one."

"Nuparu, you kolhii-head — you're dreaming!" said Hewkii, smacking his fellow Toa in the mask. "And if you don't wake up quick, you might not wake up at all."

Nuparu's eyes flashed to life. He looked around to see he was lying at the bottom of an underwater trench. Hewkii was crouched over him. The Toa of Earth adjusted his mask and said, irritated, "What did you hit me for? You know we can get out of here whenever we like."

"Good. Then tell them," Hewkii replied, gesturing over his shoulder.

Nuparu sat up and saw what his friend was

talking about. The sides of the trench were riddled with holes, each one housing a large, eyeless breed of eel. The mouth of each one was filled with more than a thousand needle-like teeth. They jutted out of their holes, craning their bodies to snap at any fish that went by. He saw one stretch almost the entire width of the trench to catch a tiny red darter, then slowly withdraw into its nest.

"Okay, climbing is out," said the Toa of Earth. "What about your mask power?"

"We won't rise fast enough," said Hewkii. "I could make them heavier, but there's an awful lot of them. I tried blocking their holes with elemental stone, but the mud's so soft, the rocks just fell down to the bottom of the trench. Before I tried anything that could get us permanently dead, I figured I'd better wake you up."

"I know a way out," said Nuparu. "But I'll need your help to make it work."

"Does it involve levers, pulleys, bits and pieces of Bohrok, or gears bigger than I am?" asked Hewkii.

"No. It involves explosions. Lots and lots of explosions."

Hewkii smiled. "Then I'm your Toa."

A few moments later, the two Toa Inika stood back to back. Hewkii shouted, "Go!" Nuparu called on his elemental power to form a column of earth beneath their feet, lifting them toward the top of the trench. As he did so, Hewkii fired his Cordak blaster at any eel that appeared, while using his stone power against the rest. His attack blew large holes in the trench, sending some of the creatures tumbling toward the bottom.

They were almost at the top when one ambitious Rahi vaulted from its hole through the water and wrapped itself around Hewkii. Off balance, the Toa of Stone tumbled off the earthen column. Nuparu spotted him just in time and grabbed Hewkii's arm, but the eel was going for its victim's throat.

"Let go!" yelled the Toa of Stone. "I can't shoot the blaster with you so close!"

"If you use it at such close range, you'll

blow your own head off!" Nuparu shouted back. He dropped his own blaster and grabbed the eel by the throat. It hissed and twisted, trying to sink its teeth into Nuparu's arm.

Hewkii took advantage of the breather to bring the power of his mask to bear. He lowered the creature's personal gravity, so that it floated up and off his body. Nuparu released his grip on the Rahi just as Hewkii used his mask again to raise and lower the gravity of the creature in specific spots, effectively tying it into a knot. Then he flung it back into the open sea.

Nuparu gave Hewkii a hand up. They had reached the top of the trench now. A welcoming committee was waiting for them: Ehlek and thirty or forty electric eels.

"All right, let's take him apart," growled Hewkii. "And when we're done down here, I don't want to see even a puddle of water ever again."

"Got a better idea," said Nuparu, smiling. "There are a few big sharks swimming way above where our friend is standing. What do you think would happen if they suddenly gained weight?"

Hewkii nodded. Once again, he used his mask, this time to increase gravity around the sharks Nuparu had spotted. Suddenly, the hunters of the sea were diving at high speed, smashing into the Barraki and the eels. The creatures responded with shocks to what they thought was an attack. Angered, the sharks attacked for real, savaging the Barraki's force in a frenzy. The two Toa could hear Ehlek cursing Pridak as he withdrew.

"You know what?" said Nuparu. "I think we just ruined a friendship."

"Yeah," agreed Hewkii, smiling. "And I'm all broken up about it."

With his strength fading, Jaller knew he had to take a desperate gamble. Reaching out blindly, he grabbed Kongu's arm and sent a blast of searing heat through both their bodies. The squid attacking them shrieked in pain and detached itself, fleeing for the open water.

The two Toa Inika staggered to their feet.

Kongu leaned on the cavern wall for support as he eyed the two Barraki. "You call yourselves warlords?" he spat. "Warlords don't quick-hide behind Rahi beasts. They do their own killing."

"We are also smart enough to tell when an enemy is trying to bait us," said Kalmah. "In our time, entire nations bowed before us . . . cities fell . . . armies were destroyed. Do you really think a group of condemned Toa will prove more than a moment's annoyance?"

Jaller stood up straight, showing none of the exhaustion he felt. "We weren't condemned here," he said. "You Barraki got it wrong."

"Why else would you be here?" said Carapar. "Nobody comes here unless they have to."

"We came from an island on the surface called Voya Nui," Jaller replied. "We're here for the Mask of Life. Help us get our hands on it, and we'll show you the way out of this place."

Kalmah laughed for a long time. It wasn't a pleasant sound. "Escape to where? Look at us,

Toa — we have been changed by this place. We can no longer live on the surface, and neither can you."

Jaller smiled. "But the mask can change that — that's what you think, isn't it? That's why you want it. We can make a deal . . . or we can fight, and risk the mask getting destroyed in the battle."

"Since when do Toa make deals?" asked Carapar, snapping his claws angrily. "Don't treat us like we're Rahi — before we wound up here, your kind lived in fear of us. Everyone did."

"Past days," said Kongu. "Is that all you have?"

"We earned the right to rule," said Kalmah quietly. "It is a right we never willingly surrendered. If we aid you now, it means going up against our allies. . . . What do you have to offer that is worth that?"

Jaller was silent for a moment. Then he said, "When the Mask of Life is back in our hands, Barraki, we'll make sure you get all you have earned and everything you deserve. Oppose us — and I swear to you by Mata Nui, we will destroy the mask before you ever get your claws on it."

The Toa of Fire waited for a response. He didn't believe for a moment the two Barraki would truly honor any bargain made between them. But if it got him and Kongu out of this cave in one piece, he would worry about the inevitable betrayal later.

"Your offer is intriguing," said Kalmah. "But promises and vows mean nothing beneath the waves. Even if we agreed, Pridak would never go along with aiding Toa. So you are going to do a favor for us in return for our assistance."

"What favor?" asked Jaller.

"Kill Pridak. Then we'll talk."

Matoro swam in the midst of a nightmare. All around him, Takea sharks were locked in battle with their reanimated victims. The carnage was mind-numbing, overwhelming, and more than a little sickening. Pridak's legions destroyed their foes, only to see them rise again through the power of the Toa's mask. And each time it happened,

Matoro felt as if he had lost another part of himself.

Is this the price the Mask of Life asks to save the Great Spirit Mata Nui? the Toa of Ice asked himself. *Already, I've seen Matoran enslaved, Piraka driven mad, Brutaka betraying everything he ever believed in, all in the name of a cursed mask. And now more death and destruction, this time through my actions. Where does it end?*

"It doesn't, you fool," said Maxilos/Makuta.

"So," said Matoro. "You are still in that body. I thought you had fled at the first sign of danger."

"It seemed like a good idea to remain silent," the Master of Shadows replied. "The Barraki and I are . . . old friends. It is an acquaintance I prefer not to renew."

"You may not have a choice. They show no sign of backing down."

"There are always choices . . . some easier than others. The Barraki made theirs eighty thousand years ago when they decided to challenge

Mata Nui. Now they are living with the consequences."

"Just like you?"

Makuta laughed through the mouth of Maxilos. "Yes, I made my choices, too. But it is not I who will have to face the consequences of them — it's you and your kind, Toa. You have not yet begun to pay the price demanded of you."

There was a sudden movement on the right flank as a school of Takea sharks slammed into Matoro's forces. His ranks were shattered by the ferocity of the attack, and the sharks shot forward before the Toa could reanimate his soldiers again. Pridak was no novice when it came to battle. He had studied Matoro's tactics and realized the key to victory was shock and speed. The Toa of Ice used his elemental power to freeze as many of the attackers as he could, but more moved in to replace them.

"You could help!" Matoro snapped at Maxilos. "You keep saying you want me to win."

"Choices, little Toa," said Maxilos. "It all comes down to choices. Unless I am mistaken, the Barraki called Ehlek has made a very bad one for himself and a very good one for us."

Now Matoro could see what Maxilos was referring to. Hundreds of thousands of eels were swimming toward the battle from the west. But when the creatures arrived, they didn't join with the sharks to attack the Toa's forces. Instead, they mobbed the Takea, overcoming the sharks with sheer numbers and scattering the schools. Within a matter of moments, the backbone of Pridak's attack was broken, destroyed by his own ally's army.

"What's going on?" asked Matoro. "I thought all the Barraki were on the same side."

"Throw a group of your enemies into the vilest prison imaginable and they will forge a stronger bond, for they are all sharing the same misery," Maxilos replied. "But offer even the glimpse of a means of escape, and they will tear each other to shreds scrambling for the exit."

Matoro said nothing. What was going on before his eyes was worse than anything he could imagine. It was the full fury of nature unleashed, yet it was not natural at all — these creatures were fighting and dying for no other reason than that two Barraki and a Toa wanted them to.

"Consider yourself lucky," said Maxilos. "It's not every day one gets to see a war begin."

EIGHT

Hours later, the Toa Inika regrouped at the sunken city. Jaller and Kongu seemed a little the worse for wear after their experience with the squid. Hahli was absent, something that had all her partners worried.

Mahri Nui was on full alert. Matoran aqua hunters had reported that the sea had gone mad. Sharks were at war with eels, keras crabs and squid were mysteriously absent from the waters, and there were unconfirmed reports of attacks by rays on anything that moved. Any creatures unlucky enough to get caught in the middle of one of the battles were killed by the combatants and then ignored. The "safe hour," that period of time when no predators stalked the seas, was no more.

"What have you done?" demanded Defilak. "We have ever-lost two of our herders and half a dozen hydruka in the last six hours! The battles come closer to the borders of Mahri Nui every moment. Is this how you protect us?"

Hewkii shrugged. "Turning them against each other seemed like a good idea. Who knew they would be so good at destroying each other?"

"It was a good idea," said Jaller. "Remember, we still need to find the mask. If the Barraki's armies tear each other to pieces, that buys us time to search."

"Is this what we've become?" asked Kongu. "Sacrificing Matoran lives, Rahi lives, just so we can quick-finish our mission? Hahli could be dead, for all we know, and all you care about —"

"Don't, just . . . don't," said Matoro. "If we fail at this, there won't be any more Matoran, or Rahi, or Hahli . . . or any of us. None of us are happy about what's been done," he added, glancing at Maxilos. "But I think we are going to have to do far worse before this is over."

A Ga-Matoran swam up to Defilak and said something quietly. Defilak nodded and turned to the Toa. "It's now a fact," he said. "The rays are on the move, heading straight for Mahri Nui. And they are being led by your Toa Hahli!"

Nocturn had been walking for how long? Hours? Days? Ehlek was not in any of his usual places, nor were his eels. Every time Nocturn tried to get a sea creature to stop and give him an idea of where to look, the creature died at his touch.

He stopped and looked down at the mask he was carrying. It was still glowing, though not as brightly as before. He wished it would just stop. The last thing one wanted in the depths of the ocean was to carry a great big light, since that would attract every predator for kios around. Why was he hauling it around again? Oh, yes, Pridak had insisted. He hated Pridak.

Maybe this is something he needs, thought Nocturn. *Maybe if I get rid of it, he will get into some kind of bad trouble. Maybe someone will even take his arm off, like he took mine.*

Nocturn paused, fumbled with the mask, and started to put it down on the sand. Then he hesitated. Pridak would know he had gotten rid of it and be enraged. He would take his anger out on Nocturn, like he said, and Pridak didn't make idle threats. Nocturn had once seen him go after another prisoner of the Pit. Pridak hadn't killed the Skakdi he was fighting, no, but just wounded his leg enough to hobble him. Then Pridak had left, knowing that the hunters of the sea would swiftly zero in on anything not able to get away. The outcome had been predictable . . . and messy.

Better hang on to it, Nocturn decided. He turned north and resumed walking when something struck his tentacle, something sharp, and made him drop the Mask of Life. He glanced down to see that there was a dagger embedded in his appendage. Annoyed, he yanked it out and turned to see who would be stupid enough to attack him.

Hydraxon hovered in the water, wrist dagger poised to throw, Cordak revolving blaster aimed right at Nocturn. "Far enough, runner," he said. "Drop the mask and surrender."

Nocturn was very confused. "You're

Hydraxon?" he said. "Back when the earthquake hit and we all escaped into the black water, Takadox killed you. I saw it. You're dead."

"I got better," Hydraxon replied. "And you're going back where you belong."

"But where we were isn't there anymore. Don't you remember? The ground shaking, the walls falling, the water flooding in . . ."

Hydraxon listened to Nocturn ramble on, but the words meant nothing to him. No such quake had ever happened, and he certainly hadn't been killed by a Barraki. Had he been the real Hydraxon, all those memories would have been too painful and real. But he was the jailer of the Pit re-created by the Mask of Life from a Po-Matoran, and made to have no doubts, no fears, no frightening recollections. All that mattered was his job.

He realized with a start that he had better get his mind back on his task. Nocturn had fired a sea squid at him and he doubted it was to provide him with a loving pet. Hydraxon hurled a razor-edged boomerang and sheared the monstrous creature in half. Even then, its tentacles still crawled across the sea floor, trying to reach him.

Before Nocturn could react, Hydraxon drew and hurled one of his back-mounted blades, knocking the squid launcher from his enemy's hand. Nocturn lashed out with his tentacle, wrapping it around Hydraxon's waist and drawing the jailer toward him. Hydraxon aimed his Cordak blaster at a nearby rock and fired, blasting it to rubble.

"Next time, it's your arm," he said coldly.

Nocturn smiled. He suddenly remembered something about his old jailer. Letting Hydraxon go, he scooped up two rocks and slammed them together as hard as he could. The sharp crack was incredibly loud, and to Hydraxon's sensitive hearing, painful. The jailer took a few steps back, trying to clear his head. Nocturn took advantage and slammed into him, knocking the blaster from his right hand and pinning his left to the sea floor. He snaked his tentacle around Hydraxon's throat.

"I'm using my arm right now, sorry,"

Nocturn said. "But thanks for all the weapons — I'll take them off your body when you're dead again."

"Start with this one," said Hydraxon, mentally triggering his other back blade. It arced up into the water and came down, pinning Nocturn's tentacle to the ocean floor. Hydraxon seized the moment to bring a leg up and kick Nocturn off of him. Then the jailer drew back his arm, ready to hurl a wrist blade right at Nocturn.

"I'm here to bring you back," Hydraxon said. "It really makes no difference to me if some of your parts don't make the trip."

Nocturn's shoulders slumped. Keeping an eye on his captive, Hydraxon stepped around him and picked up the glowing Kanohi mask. The part of him that was the jailer of the Pit knew this mask must be important if the Barraki wanted it, and it should probably be kept safe and away from them. But a smaller part of him, the remnants of Dekar's consciousness, remembered this mask as something dangerous and destructive. In the wrong hands, the Mask of Life was a potentially devastating weapon. One glance at it showed it was already in the process of destroying itself. The best way to ensure it would never pose a threat would be to help it on its way.

Hydraxon gently placed the Mask of Life on the ocean floor. Then he took careful aim with his Cordak blaster, and fired.

"What if we can't find the Mask of Life in time?" Matoro said. He was swimming alongside Maxilos/Makuta, heading for the last reported sighting of Mantax's army and Toa Hahli. The other Toa Inika were spread out around them, too far away to hear.

"Ah, if only all Toa had words like 'can't' in their vocabulary," said Maxilos. "My path in life would have been much easier. I thought your kind thrived on being optimistic to the point of insanity?"

"I just asked a question," Matoro snapped.

"To which you know the answer — if Mata Nui dies, the universe that you, and I, and all your little Matoran friends know will be no more. Jaller will lose his chance to live up to the legacy of Lhikan, Vakama, Tahu, and all those other lukewarm Toa of Fire . . . Hewkii will never see his friend Macku again . . . and you? You will know that in Turaga Nuju's last moments, he branded you a failure."

When Matoro did not reply, Maxilos continued. "When this is all over, I really must retrieve my Kanohi Mask of Shadows. Those idiot Piraka let it fall into the sea near Metru Nui. Most think it just allows me to spread physical darkness, or breed a little rage here and there, but it's much more than that. My Kanohi lets me see the darkness inside everyone, all the nasty little things they hide in the shadows of their spirit. I miss that . . . of course, I hardly need it with you, Matoro. Yours are practically written on your mask."

Matoro looked over his shoulder at Maxilos. "Let me tell you something — if the universe ends, if everyone and everything is going to die . . . I'm going to make sure you die first."

Maxilos laughed. "You wouldn't want that. After all, if anything happens to me, you will never know what to do with the Mask of Life when you get it —'when,' Toa, not 'if.' I have no intention of letting you fail."

He's bluffing, thought Matoro. *He doesn't have any more idea what to do with that mask than we do. He just wants to make sure I don't try freezing him solid from the inside out.*

"If you know so much, then tell me — if we get the Mask of Life from the Barraki, then what?" asked the Toa of Ice.

"I would think it would be obvious," Maxilos said impatiently. "All must be as it was for Mata Nui to be healed. That means Voya Nui cannot remain floating above us like some discarded Matoran tool. Once the mask is in your hands, you will need to destroy the stone cord linking Voya Nui to Mahri Nui, the cord you passed through to reach this place."

"And then?"

"Pessimistic *and* dense — you truly set a new standard for Toa," Maxilos replied sharply. "Then Voya Nui will return to where it came from. Of course, anyone living on it will be killed in the process . . . and Mahri Nui will be completely destroyed, along with its occupants. Acceptable losses to save the universe, wouldn't you agree?"

Seeing Matoro's grim expression, the master of shadows patted him on the back. "Cheer up, little Toa. When all is said and done, and two islands' worth of Matoran are dead, your name will live in history — right alongside mine."

EPILOGUE

Far to the north, six other heroes were facing troubles of their own.

At one time, these six Toa were known as Toa Mata, named for the Great Spirit Mata Nui, whose welfare was their primary mission. Now they were Toa Nuva, transformed by fate into more powerful heroes. Right now, they were very confused heroes as well.

"This is nuts," said Pohatu Nuva. "The action is back with Matoro and the rest, fighting to save Mata Nui's life. And where are we? Trekking back to our old stomping grounds because some kook with an ax says we should."

"Worse than that," added Kopaka Nuva, Toa of Ice, "is what he wants us to do when we get there. How do we know we can trust this Axonn character? What if this is all a trick?"

Tahu Nuva, leader of the team, wished

there was not so much truth in what Kopaka said. After being freed from their imprisonment on the island of Voya Nui, the Toa Nuva had fully intended to join with the Toa Inika in their quest for the Mask of Life. Instead, they had run into two strange beings — one called Axonn, the other Botar — who informed them that a number of dangerous quests required their attention. They were the only ones who could do them, it was part of their destiny, but they had to leave now. And the first of these meant returning to the city of Metru Nui. Faced with the urgency of the situation, they had taken Toa transport canisters back to the outskirts of that island metropolis. Now they moved quietly through darkened streets, trying to avoid being seen.

"It makes no sense to me, either," Tahu Nuva said finally. "But Axonn helped the Matoran and the Toa Inika on that island, and he claims to know the will of Mata Nui. We will take him at his word, until we have reason to do otherwise."

"Right," Pohatu said sarcastically. "The Great Beings know Toa are never deceived."

"We're taking a risk, maybe a big one," Tahu replied. "And if it turns out we've been misled, then we have the power to deal with that . . . and with Axonn, too."

Their argument had brought them to their destination, the recently rebuilt Great Temple in the Ga-Metru district. Destroyed by quake and fire 1,000 years before, it had largely been restored by the hard work of the Ga-Matoran. It was filled with some of the most ancient and valuable artifacts known to the villagers, kept there (or hidden there) for safekeeping. Tonight would test whether one such artifact was safe from the Toa.

"Can't we just go to the Turaga and ask for what we need?" said Gali Nuva. "Is this mission so important it must turn us into thieves?"

"You know what would result, Gali — endless debate," said Onua, Toa Nuva of Earth. "And in the end, unless we tell them how we know what we know, they will never agree. Makuta bones, we're the ones doing this, and we don't even agree on it!"

Lewa Nuva slashed his hand through the air. "Enough dark-talk, unless we want the Matoran to hear. We're close enough now."

"Then do it, Lewa," said Tahu.

The Toa Nuva of Air nodded and triggered the power of his Kanohi Mask of Speed. Being a Nuva mask, its power could be shared with other beings in the vicinity. In a split second, all six Toa Nuva were now gifted with amazing speed. They took off at a run, flashing past the Ga-Matoran guards, too fast to be seen. Nor did they pause to open the temple gate, but simply vibrated their atoms so they could pass right through the massive door. They did not slow down until they were inside.

"From Toa to sneak thief, in one easy lesson," Pohatu grumbled. "Maybe when this is over we should see if the Dark Hunters have any openings."

"This way," said Gali, leading them through the corridors and into a large, empty chamber.

"There's nothing here," said Kopaka. "We

have been misled. This Axonn simply wanted us off Voya Nui for his own purposes."

"You've grown too used to wearing a Mask of Vision, brother," Gali chided. "You insist on seeing with your eyes. If our information is correct, there is more to this room than is plainly visible."

She took three strides toward the center of the room, one to the left, two more forward, and then two to the right. "Here, Pohatu. This block of stone requires your attention."

The Toa of Stone joined Gali. Bending over, Pohatu grabbed the part of the floor she pointed to, sinking his powerful fingers into the rock. Then he effortlessly pulled the block free.

All six Toa gathered around to see what was there. After a moment's stunned silence, Gali reached in and retrieved the unfamiliar object. It consisted of two short, round staffs made of wood, and rolled around them was a thin white sheet of a substance none of the Toa had seen before.

"Odd," said Kopaka. "What do you think it is?"

"Axonn said we would find a vital message," Tahu said. "I expected a carving of some sort."

Gali shifted the object in her hands, and it suddenly unrolled. Now all six Toa Nuva could see that there was Matoran writing on the sheet, just like the language found carved into stone tablets all over Metru Nui. But this was not carved, rather it was painted onto the sheet in some way.

"Well, that's dumb," said Pohatu. "Why use this when there are perfectly good rocks everywhere you look?"

"We can worry about their choice of stationery later," said Kopaka. "I am still trying to digest what this says. Is it some kind of monstrous joke?"

"Do you hear anyone laughing?" Tahu replied. "It says these actions must be taken to wake the Great Spirit. But some of what it asks . . . how can we be expected to do such things?"

"No one said being a Toa hero would be a bowl of bula berries," said Lewa. "Now let's get out of here — it looks like we have a lot of unpleasant work to do."

The first item on the scroll was, on the face of it, the easiest . . . and at the same time, one of the hardest for the heroes to bring themselves to do.

A journey of several hours had brought them to their destination, the site of their first major battle as Toa Nuva. Here in this rock-hewn chamber, they had battled enemies called Bohrok-Kal to keep even greater threats imprisoned. Now they were here to set two of their most powerful opponents free.

The Bahrag were still where the Toa had left them, imprisoned in a cage of solid protodermis. When they were free, they had led the Bohrok swarms who threatened to devastate the island of Mata Nui. For reasons that we never clear, the Bohrok were determined to destroy every mountain, forest, and river, and return the island to a barren state. But the Toa had beaten them and the Bahrag and saved Mata Nui and the Matoran from that fate.

"And now we're just supposed to let them go?" demanded Pohatu Nuva. "Check that list again; maybe Makuta signed his name at the bottom."

"Pohatu's exaggerating . . . maybe," said Gali Nuva. "But, Tahu, how can this be the right thing to do?"

"Axonn said everything was not how it seemed," said the Toa Nuva of Fire. "If this will somehow help the Great Spirit to awaken, then we have to do it."

"And if it doesn't?" asked Lewa Nuva.

"Then we beat the swarms before, and we'll beat them again," Tahu replied. "Now join your powers with mine."

Hesitantly, the six Toa Nuva pooled their [illegible] [illegible]nt them out in a single beam. It [illegible] Toa seal that kept the prison intact, and seconds later, the cage itself had collapsed. The Bahrag were free once more.

"Why have you released us?" asked one of the two monstrosities.

"Because someone we . . . trust . . . says it is the order of things," Tahu Nuva replied. "The Bohrok were not meant to be on the island when they were, and so had to be beaten back. But now . . ."

Tahu stopped, remembering the whole-scale destruction of the last swarm attack. No, he couldn't bring himself to say the words, even if Axonn was correct. He couldn't believe the Great Spirit would want this.

"Now the signal will be given," Onua Nuva said. Tahu turned to look at the Toa Nuva of Earth, but Onua's eyes were focused on the Bahrag. "The Bohrok will be awakened, and they will carry out their task. Do you understand?"

"We do," said the Bahrag in unison. "The island of Mata Nui shall be as it was in the before-time."

"What have you done?" Pohatu Nuva said,

mask to mask with Onua Nuva. "We have to cage those two up again — now!"

Onua Nuva shook his head. "I believe I've done what I had to do," he said. "I've taken the first step toward the future. No one ever said the trip would be an easy one."

The air was suddenly filled with a shrill sonic tone — and in countless nests, hundreds of thousands of Bohrok came to life, ready to resume their mission of destruction.